RACIAL JUSTICE IN AMERICA

HISTORIES

JUNETEENTH

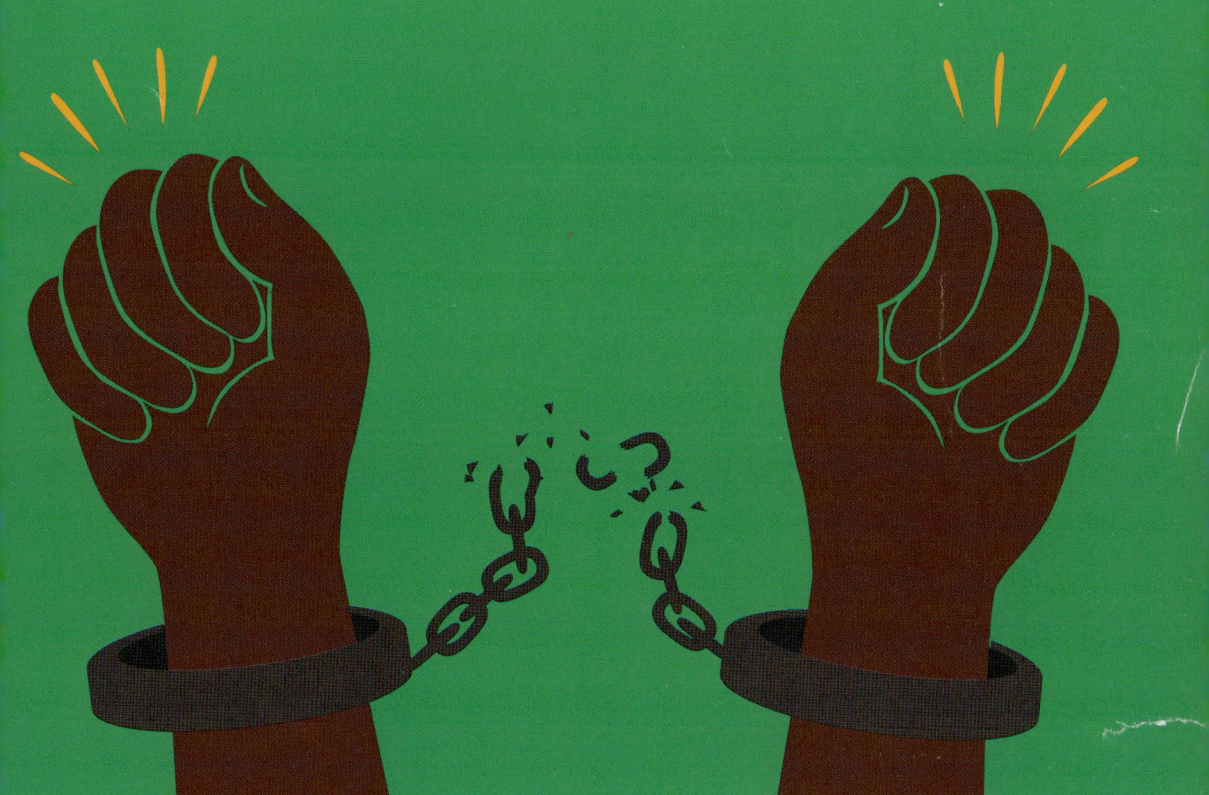

KEVIN P. WINN WITH KELISA WING

Cherry Lake Press

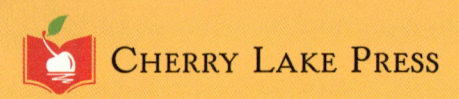

Published in the United States of America by Cherry Lake Publishing Group
Ann Arbor, Michigan
www.cherrylakepublishing.com

Reading Adviser: Beth Walker Gambro, MS, Ed., Reading Consultant, Yorkville, IL
Content Adviser: Kelisa Wing
Book Design and Cover Art: Felicia Macheske

Photo Credits: Library of Congress/Cartes de Visite Photo by Heard & Moseley, Artist unknown, LOC Control No.: 98501210, 5; Library of Congress/Photo by Detroit Publishing Co., LOC Control No.: 2016804723, 7; Library of Congress/Lithograph by E. Herline, LOC Control No.: 2004667979, 9; Unidentified U.S. Civil War Soldiers: Library of Congress/William A. Gladstone collection of African American photographs Ambrotype/Tintype, LOC Control Nos.: 2002719392 (top left), 2002719397 (top center), 2017648729 (top right), 2002719394 (bottom left), 13; Unidentified U.S. Civil War Soldiers: Library of Congress/Liljenquist Family Collection of Civil War Photographs, LOC Control Nos.: 2011661479 (middle left), 2012646977, (middle center), 2010648968 (middle right), 2012650006 (bottom center), 2010650374 (bottom right), 13; Library of Congress/Photo by Berry, Kelley, & Chadwick, Publishers, LOC Control No.: 00652640, 15; © Everett Collection/Shutterstock, 17; © FLHC A12 / Alamy Stock Photo, 18; Library of Congress/Photo by Peter P. Jones, LOC Control No.: 2013649123, 21; © yhelfman/Shutterstock, 23; © Tippman98x/Shutterstock, 24; © fitzcrittle/Shutterstock, 27; © Antwon McMullen/Shutterstock, 29

Graphics Throughout: © debra hughes/Shutterstock.com; © Natewimon Nantiwat/Shutterstock.com

Copyright © 2022 by Cherry Lake Publishing Group

All rights reserved. No part of this book may be reproduced or utilized in any form or by any means without written permission from the publisher.

Cherry Lake Press is an imprint of Cherry Lake Publishing Group.

Library of Congress Cataloging-in-Publication Data

Names: Winn, Kevin P., author. | Wing, Kelisa, author.
Title: Juneteenth / written by Kevin P. Winn, Kelisa Wing.
Description: Ann Arbor, Michigan : Cherry Lake Publishing, [2022]
 | Series: Racial justice in America: histories | Includes index. | Audience: Grades 4-6 | Summary: "The Racial Justice in America: Histories series explores moments and eras in America's history that have been ignored or misrepresented in education due to racial bias. Juneteenth explores the history around the celebration in a comprehensive, honest, and age-appropriate way. Developed in conjunction with educator, advocate, and author Kelisa Wing to reach children of all races and encourage them to approach our history with open eyes and minds. Books include 21st Century Skills and content, as well as activities created by Wing. Also includes a table of contents, glossary, index, author biography, sidebars, educational matter, and activities"— Provided by publisher.
Identifiers: LCCN 2021010812 (print) | LCCN 2021010813 (ebook) | ISBN 9781534187481 (hardcover)
 | ISBN 9781534188884 (paperback) | ISBN 9781534190283 (pdf) | ISBN 9781534191686 (ebook)
Subjects: LCSH: Juneteenth—Juvenile literature. | African Americans—Texas—History—Juvenile literature. | Slaves—Emancipation—United States—Juvenile literature. | African Americans—Anniversaries, etc.—Juvenile literature.
Classification: LCC E185.93.T4 W57 2022 (print) | LCC E185.93.T4 (ebook)
 | DDC 394.263—dc23
LC record available at https://lccn.loc.gov/2021010812
LC ebook record available at https://lccn.loc.gov/2021010813

Cherry Lake Publishing Group would like to acknowledge the work of the Partnership for 21st Century Learning, a Network of Battelle for Kids. Please visit http://www.battelleforkids.org/networks/p21 for more information.

Printed in the United States of America

Kevin P. Winn is a children's book writer and researcher. He focuses on issues of racial justice and educational equity in his work. In 2020, Kevin earned his doctorate in Educational Policy and Evaluation from Arizona State University.

Kelisa Wing honorably served in the U.S. Army and has been an educator for 14 years. She is the author of *Promises and Possibilities: Dismantling the School to Prison Pipeline*, *If I Could: Lessons for Navigating an Unjust World*, and *Weeds & Seeds: How to Stay Positive in the Midst of Life's Storms*. She speaks both nationally and internationally about discipline reform, equity, and student engagement. Kelisa lives in Northern Virginia with her husband and two children.

Chapter 1
What Is Juneteenth? | Page 4

Chapter 2
Slavery and the Emancipation Proclamation | Page 8

Chapter 3
After the Civil War | Page 14

Chapter 4
Celebrating Juneteenth through History | Page 20

Chapter 5
Juneteenth Today: Its Meaning and Its Legacy | Page 28

SHOW WHAT YOU KNOW | Page 31

Extend Your Learning | Page 32

Glossary | Page 32

Index | Page 32

CHAPTER 1

What Is Juneteenth?

June 19th.

This is an important day to know. It is the day that celebrates the freedom of the last enslaved people in the United States. They were freed on June 19, 1865, in Galveston, Texas. This was 2 months after the Civil War ended, but Black people in Texas had not yet heard the news that they were free. One reason was because the information was withheld by those who benefited from enslaved people. Plus, there were no telephones or computers. Information and news passed across the country slowly.

President Abraham Lincoln signed the order that freed enslaved people in the United States on January 1, 1863.

Juneteenth is celebrated in many communities around the United States. It **commemorates** the strength of Black people. The day is held in remembrance that Black people **persevered** even during the brutality of slavery. It's a reminder that they succeeded despite laws that worked against them. They continued to fight and to resist **White supremacy**.

Juneteenth is a reminder that Black people continue to persist in a racist country.

There are other days that have been proposed to celebrate freedom from enslavement. June 19th, or Juneteenth, is the longest-standing celebration of **emancipation**. Although not all Black people celebrate it, the day is a significant one in U.S. history.

Men, women, and children gather for an Emancipation Day celebration in Richmond, Virginia, in 1905.

CHAPTER 2
Slavery and the Emancipation Proclamation

The United States was built with enslaved people's labor. Enslaved people came from different parts of Africa. Many Africans were captured and sold against their wills to White Americans and Europeans. In 1807, the Abolition of the Slave Trade Act passed. This made trading enslaved people illegal between continents, but it did nothing to stop slavery in the United States. In fact, the United States was one of the few countries in the world where enslaved people were expected to reproduce. Children of slaves were born into slavery.

The United States was divided by slavery. **Abolitionists** were people who fought against the evils of slavery. Their views were popular in the North. By 1804, all Northern states abolished slavery. This idea was not popular in the South, where owners of large farms used enslaved people to do the work. This disagreement led to the Civil War.

The United States grew more divided when South Carolina **seceded** from the North—also called the Union. State leaders claimed the federal government didn't have the right to tell South Carolina what to do. Other Southern states agreed. They followed South Carolina's lead. By 1861, 11 states left the Union. They formed their own country called the Confederate States of America, or Confederacy. Confederate troops attacked Fort Sumter in South Carolina on April 12, 1861. The Civil War had begun.

The South seceded from the United States over laws against using enslaved people for labor.

Abraham Lincoln was the president of the United States at the time. He didn't want the country to be divided. He would have done anything to save it. Although he is celebrated, he was not always the abolitionist the history books teach. In a letter in 1862, he stated, "My **paramount** object in this struggle is to save the Union, and is not either to save or destroy Slavery. If I could save the Union without freeing any slave, I would do it, and if I could save it by freeing all the slaves, I would do it, and if I could save it by freeing some and leaving others alone, I would also do that. What I do about Slavery and the colored race, I do because I believe it helps to save this Union." Why does this context matter? It is important because it shows his reasoning for the language of the Emancipation Proclamation.

Abraham Lincoln issued the Emancipation Proclamation. It took effect on January 1, 1863. The proclamation declared that enslaved people in the Confederacy were free. What did that actually mean? Although the proclamation sounded promising, there were holes in the law. Remember when Lincoln said that he would do anything to preserve the Union? Well, he did just that. His proclamation was only for enslaved people in the Confederate states. It said nothing about Union states that still held enslaved people. This meant that states like Maryland, which was still part of the Union but hadn't outlawed slavery, didn't have to free its enslaved people.

Words Matter

Using the term "enslaved person" instead of "slave" gives people who are held in captivity the humanity and dignity they deserve. Nobody is simply a slave. They are a human first and foremost. Enslaving other humans is wrong, cruel, and unjust.

Because the Northern Union states were fighting against Confederate states during the Civil War, Lincoln couldn't enforce the Emancipation Proclamation. Confederate President Jefferson Davis didn't agree with freeing enslaved people, so they remained enslaved.

The Emancipation Proclamation *was* important. Although it couldn't be enforced in the Confederacy, it was a symbol of hope. It helped convince freed Black people to fight in the North against the South. In fact, nearly 200,000 Black people, including formerly enslaved people, fought for the Union against the Confederacy. Their service was essential for the North to succeed and eventually win against the South.

When Black people were finally allowed to join the Civil War in 1862, they still faced discrimination. They often were not allowed to fight. Instead, they served in positions like carpenters, cooks, and scouts. Until 1864, they also received less money than White soldiers.

Over 180,000 Black men served in the Civil War.

CHAPTER 3

After the Civil War

The Civil War ended on April 9, 1865. Confederate General Robert E. Lee surrendered to Union General Ulysses S. Grant. The Confederacy no longer existed. The 11 states that seceded returned to the Union.

Not everyone heard that the war was over right away. Slavery continued in the southwest in the state of Texas. Two months after the war, General Gordon Granger, who represented the Union, arrived in Texas. He announced that the war was over. All 250,000 enslaved people in Texas were free. This was on June 19th, which came to be known as Juneteenth.

But even then, some enslaved people didn't hear the news until after June 19th. Historians believe that White people worked hard to keep the announcement a secret. They wanted to keep enslaved people working for them for free for at least another harvest season.

White plantation owners benefited financially from the institution of slavery. They did not want to see it end.

In 1866, the first Juneteenth celebration occurred in Texas. It was one year after slavery officially ended. It was also during a period called **Reconstruction**. During the Civil War, much of the South was destroyed. Cities needed to be rebuilt. People needed jobs and homes. The North decided to help. During Reconstruction, Black people gained freedom and rights. The United States added three new amendments to the Constitution. The Thirteenth Amendment outlawed slavery. The Fourteenth said all people born or **naturalized** in the United States were citizens. The Fifteenth allowed all men, including Black men, to vote. At the time, women weren't allowed to vote.

When Reconstruction ended in 1877, White people worked to eliminate any gains Black people had made.

Reconstruction lasted only until 1877. Although Black people had gained freedoms and rights, they were still targeted by racists. Even their Juneteenth celebrations were forbidden by racists who thought Black people didn't deserve to celebrate.

They put laws into place to restrict Black people's freedoms. These were called Black codes. These codes monitored Black people's every movement. It made many things illegal for Black people, such as holding high-paying jobs. The Black codes were further developed into official laws in Southern states. For example, Mississippi adopted a new state constitution. It said that Black people had to pass a *literacy* test if they wanted to vote. Many were formerly enslaved people who had never attended school. They couldn't read or write. In this way, White people tried to force Black people back into slavery.

Trying to restrict Black people from voting or joining government was a way for White people to control Black people.

Families gather for a Juneteenth celebration in Texas in 1900.

Even among these difficulties, formerly enslaved people found ways to celebrate their freedoms. It was important to them to commemorate their new rights. It also made a strong statement in this time and place. Texas was a Southern state that eventually adopted Jim Crow segregation—a form of law that kept White and Black people separate from one another. By going against White Southerners' wishes, Black people stood up for and advocated for themselves. In fact, White people wouldn't let Black people celebrate their freedom on White-owned land. Many of the first Juneteenth celebrations occurred in rural areas near lakes and rivers.

CHAPTER 4

Celebrating Juneteenth through History

Juneteenth celebrations have included a range of activities throughout their history. They continue to develop as time progresses. In the beginning, many of the celebrations, which started in Texas, had a spiritual aspect. Some took place at churches. They also included food and song, but one thing is clear. They were mainly occasions to celebrate how Black people have continued to fight against constant injustice and unfairness in the United States.

Although many formerly enslaved people had no belongings, they worked hard to earn money after slavery ended. They saved what they made. By 1872, formerly enslaved people pooled their money. They successfully bought 10 acres (4 hectares) of land in

Houston, Texas, for $1,000. They transformed that land into a park. Today, it's called Emancipation Park. Houston's yearly Juneteenth celebrations are held there. Black people also bought another plot of land in Mexia, Texas. They called it Booker T. Washington Park, after the famous Black teacher and leader.

Booker T. Washington founded Tuskegee University, which today is a top-ranked Historically Black College and University (HBCU).

Juneteenth is the longest-running celebration of emancipation from enslavement, but the celebrations slowed down for a while during the 1940s. The tradition to celebrate wasn't always passed down, and many people didn't know what Juneteenth was. However, Juneteenth celebrations made a comeback when states like Texas worked to make it a holiday. More people began learning about the day and its importance.

Black abolitionist and speaker Frederick Douglass saw the importance of celebrating the freedom of enslaved people. In talking about Fourth of July—or Independence Day—celebrations, he said, "This Fourth of July is yours, not mine. You may rejoice, I must mourn." He mourned because Black people were not free in the United States.

People who were freed from slavery used red, black, and green to represent their freedom. Red for the blood that had been shed. Black for the color of their skin. And green for the land they stood free upon.

Juneteenth is a way for Black Americans to celebrate their history and honor their past while enjoying their families and community.

People celebrate Juneteenth in different ways. Families and friends gather for prayers and celebration. Poems are written and recited. Speeches, music, and dancing take place. Many people celebrate with food, often barbecue. It is said that barbecue allows people to share in the scents that their enslaved ancestors experienced. Black people often only had access to the meat White people didn't want. Barbecue became the preferred method of cooking the tough meats. These foods symbolize the **resilience** and strength of enslaved people surviving under the horrors of slavery.

Aspects of teaching are also incorporated into Juneteenth celebrations. People read the Emancipation Proclamation and General Granger's announcement of freedom for all enslaved people in Texas. The celebrations also change with the times. Modern celebrations may include parades, baseball and basketball games, storytelling, and music.

The symbolism of Juneteenth continues with its flag. The flag's colors are red, white, and blue—just like the U.S. flag. These colors were chosen to represent that enslaved people and their descendants were American and deserved rights just like every other American citizen. The middle features a single bursting star. The one star represents Texas—the Lone Star state—but also all U.S. states. The burst symbolizes new freedom. It bursts over a line—a horizon—to show there are new opportunities in the future for Black people.

June 19, 1865

What do the colors and design of the American flag symbolize?
How is it different from this flag?

27

CHAPTER 5

Juneteenth Today: Its Meaning and Its Legacy

Many Americans are unaware of Juneteenth. It's not mentioned in most history books, but it remains important. People are working hard to make sure it is recognized. In 1979, Texas became the first state to recognize it as a holiday. Now, 47 states and Washington, D.C., recognize it as a holiday.

Activists don't think this is enough. They are working to make Juneteenth a federal holiday. They explain that it's important for the United States to recognize its racist history. Other countries have done this as well. For example, in places like Germany, many cities have monuments to Jewish people murdered in the

Holocaust. It is a daily recognition of those who suffered and died. Remembering is also a way to ensure that we never forget our past. Forgetting history makes it easier to repeat it.

Remembering Juneteenth, and the circumstances that led to it, means we won't forget the injustices Black Americans have faced.

Texas was the first state to make Juneteenth a paid holiday. Al Edwards, a Black member of Congress from Houston, worked to pass this bill. He was a lifelong antiracist activist. He protested during the civil rights movement and later during South Africa's unfair apartheid system. Al Edwards died on April 29, 2020, and is remembered as Mr. Juneteenth.

Knowledge of Juneteenth is growing. Unfortunately, it often takes tragedies for the celebration to receive its proper recognition. This was especially true after George Floyd, an unarmed Black man, was murdered by police in Minnesota. His murder was filmed, and people across the world saw the horrors of continued racism on video. Protests against police brutality occurred, and Americans worked to learn more about the country's racist past. Progress includes learning more, but also celebrating the constant resilience and perseverance of Black Americans in the face of racism. This is done through remembering and celebrating Juneteenth.

SHOW WHAT YOU KNOW

Do you know what emigration is? Emigration means to leave one's own country in order to settle permanently in another. As Abraham Lincoln struggled with what to do with freed enslaved people, he proposed emigrating them to Liberia in Africa. Lincoln thought this might solve the struggles involved in freeing Black people and making them equal to White people. Ultimately, he proposed for freed enslaved people, who were born in the United States, to leave. This story isn't commonly found in history books because many people remember President Lincoln only for the good he did. However, it is important to know the whole story of American history.

For this show what you know assignment, research what emigration is and President Lincoln's proposal and plans for emigration. How might this plan have negatively impacted Black people? Why is it important to be honest about the good and bad things people have done in our history?

Do you know there are so many different ways to show what you know? Rather than using traditional ways to display knowledge, try something new to complete this assignment. Here are some ideas:

1. Rap
2. Mural
3. Musical
4. Debate
5. Web page
6. Speech
7. Bulletin board
8. Jigsaw puzzle
9. Show and tell
10. Essay
11. Diorama
12. Performance
13. Podcast
14. Journal
15. OR add your own...

EXTEND YOUR LEARNING

Nasheed, Jameelah, "Why We Should All Be Celebrating Juneteenth," *Teen Vogue*, June 19, 2019, www.teenvogue.com/story/juneteenth-celebration-meaning-explainer

GLOSSARY

abolitionists (ah-buh-LIH-shuh-nists) people who fought against slavery

activists (AK-tih-vistz) people who work for a cause

apartheid (uh-PAHR-tyt) a system of laws in South Africa that separated people of different races

commemorates (kuh-MEH-muh-rayts) remembers or celebrates

emancipation (ih-man-suh-PAY-shuhn) freedom from something

Holocaust (HOL-uh-kahst) the mass killing of Jewish people in Europe during World War II

literacy (lih-tuh-ruh-see) the ability to read and write

naturalized (NAH-chuh-ruh-lyzd) a person who is allowed to become a citizen

paramount (PA-ruh-mownt) the most important

persevered (pur-suh-VEERD) continued trying even when times are tough

Reconstruction (ree-kuhn-STRUK-shuhn) the period after the Civil War when Southern states were rebuilding and Black people had more rights

resilience (ri-ZIL-yuhns) strength during difficult times

seceded (sih-SEED-uhd) formally left an organization or group

White supremacy (WITE suh-PREH-muh-see) the incorrect belief that White people and their ideas are superior to all others

INDEX

Abolition of the Slave Trade Act, 8
abolitionists, 8, 10, 22

barbecue, 25
Black codes, 16–17
Black people. *See also* freed Black people
 buy land for park in Houston, 20–21
 discrimination against, 12
 fight against injustice and unfairness, 20
 persistence of, 6, 30
 soldiers, 13
 voting rights, 17
Booker T. Washington Park, 21

Civil War
 beginning of, 9
 Black people join, 12
 end of, 4, 14
 Reconstruction period, 14–19
 and slavery, 8
 soldiers, 13
Confederacy, 9, 11, 14
Constitution, U.S., 16

Davis, Jefferson, 12
discrimination, 12
Douglass, Frederick, 22

Edwards, Al, 30
emancipation, 6, 7
Emancipation Proclamation
 issued, 11
 language of, 10
 Lincoln's inability to enforce, 12
 as part of Juneteenth celebrations, 25
 and slavery, 8–13
 as symbol of hope, 12
emigration, 31
enslaved people, 11
 celebrate freedoms, 19
 and Emancipation Proclamation, 8–13
 freed in Texas, 4, 14–15

Fifteenth Amendment, 16
flag, 26, 27
Floyd, George, 30
Fort Sumter, 9
Fourteenth Amendment, 16
freed Black people, 12, 17, 31

Galveston, TX, 4
Granger, Gordon, 14, 25
Grant, Ulysses S., 14

Houston, TX, 20–21

Independence Park, 20–21
Jim Crow segregation, 19

Juneteenth, 14
 celebrations, 6, 19, 20–27
 first celebration of, 16
 flag, 26, 27
 meaning and legacy, 28–30
 as official holiday, 28
 what it is, 4–7

Lee, Robert E., 14
Liberia, 31
Lincoln, Abraham, 10–11, 12, 31
literacy tests, 17

Mississippi, 17

Northern states. *See* Union

racism, 6, 16, 28, 30
Reconstruction, 14–19
Richmond, VA, 7

secession, 9
segregation, 19
slaves/slavery, 8, 16. *See also* enslaved people
South Carolina, 9
Southern states. *See also* Confederacy
 pass laws to restrict Black people's freedoms, 17
 use of enslaved people, 8

Texas, 4, 14
 and Jim Crow segregation, 19
 Juneteenth celebrations, 16, 20, 22
 recognizes Juneteenth as holiday, 28, 30
Thirteenth Amendment, 16

Union, 8–12, 14
United States
 divided by slavery, 8
 racist history, 28, 30

voting, 17

Washington, Booker T., 21
White people
 attempts to restrict Black people's freedoms, 16–17
 supremacy of, 6

32